Steadman S... Plays Basketball

Written by Jeffrey Roy Ford

Illustrations by Mike Motz

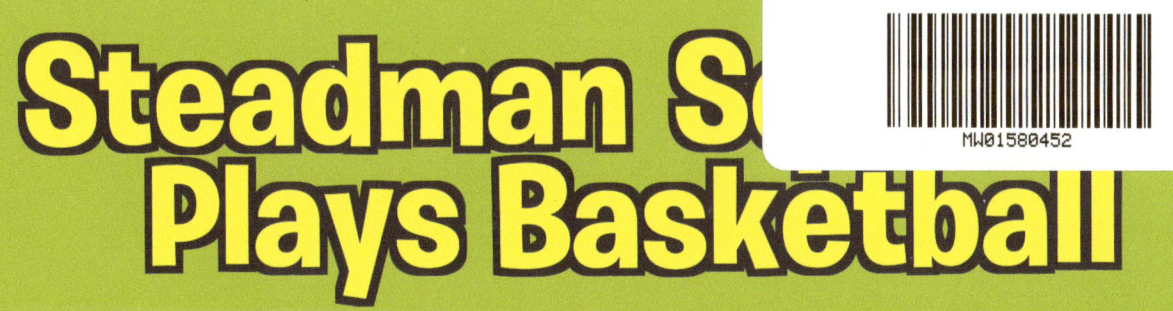

I dedicate this book to God,
my family, and my friends.

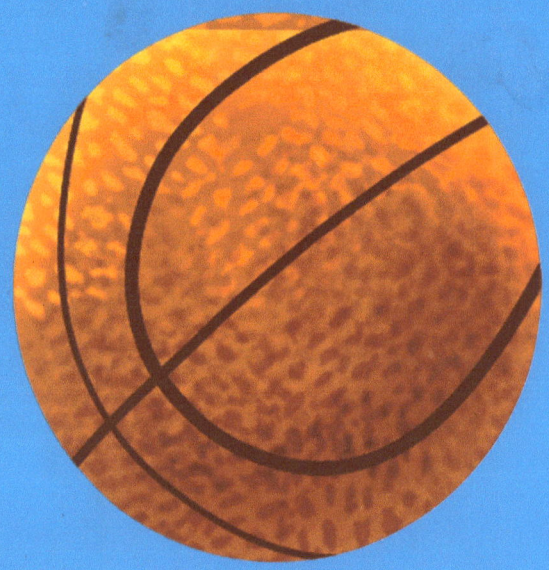

Steadman Squirrel Plays Basketball
© 2022 Jeffrey Roy Ford. All Rights reserved.
No part of this publication may be reproduced or transmitted in any form
or by any means, electronic, mechanical, including photocopy,
recording, or any information storage and retrieval system,
without permission in writing from the author.

Steadman Squirrel Plays Basketball

Written by Jeffrey Roy Ford

Illustrations by Mike Motz

"Pass the ball, Steadman!" Rashawn Racoon shouts.

Steadman Squirrel and Rashawn Racoon are playing in the Banana Nut Creek Elementary School's 2-on-2 Basketball Tournament championship game.

Pernell and Paxton Possum are guarding Steadman, while his teammate, Rashawn, is wide open near the basketball rim.

"Pass me the ball, Steadman!" Rashawn shouts again.

Steadman ignores him. He looks at his friends, Rema Rabbit and Kamari Kitty, cheering for him in the crowd full of students in the bleachers of the school's gym.

With sweat dripping down his blue jersey and his heart beating fast, he wiggles his bushy tail and braces himself. He jumps and shoots the basketball over both defenders and scores, winning the game.

"I won! I did it!" Steadman cheers. The students run onto the basketball court and surround Steadman. They jump for joy as they celebrate the victory.

They lift him in the air, cheering his name. "Steadman! Steadman!"

"I did it! I won the game!" Steadman screams.

Rashawn frowns as no one pays any attention to him. "I helped out too," he says.

After the game, Rema, Kamari, Steadman, and Rashawn walk down the nature trail of Freshy Forest.

"Steadman, you were great!" Kamari mentions.

Steadman smiles. "I am such a natural at basketball. I can't wait to tell my parents that I won the game!"

Rashawn puts his head down and kicks an acorn into the blueberry bushes. "What about me, guys? I scored some points too."

The children walk by Freshy River. They see Professor Ozello Owl and Dr. Billy Bobcat on top of Ozello's treehouse, fixing his roof.

"I finally patched in the last hole," Dr. Billy Bobcat says.

"Ha! Ha! You fixed my roof. Thank you!" Professor Ozello Owl exclaims.

"No, Ozello, we did it! You helped out too," Dr. Billy Bobcat responds.

The children arrive outside Steadman's home, and Steadman immediately climbs up the oak tree and goes inside.

"Momma! Papa! I made the game-winning basket. I won the championship game all by myself," he announces.

Rashawn overhears Steadman talking to his parents. He puts his paws over his furry face, and tears pour from his eyes. "Why isn't Steadman giving me any credit?"

Rema puts her arm around him. "Rashawn, it will be okay."

The next day at school, Steadman and his little brother, Stewart, walk inside the school's cafeteria, and the students immediately give him a round of applause.

"Steadman! Steadman!" they cheer. Steadman smiles, raising his paws in the air as he gloats.

"Oink! Oink! Stewart! Stop dancing on the table!" Principal Pandra Pig yells.

Steadman goes over to a brown wooden table where Rashawn and Rema are sitting. "Rashawn, everyone loves me. Let's sign up and play in next year's tournament."

Rashawn grunts and turns away from Steadman, sticking his wet nose in the air. "No! I don't want to play with you anymore. You don't give me any credit!"

Steadman runs out of the cafeteria with tears in his eyes.

Mr. Dorian Dog follows him. "Woof! Woof! Steadman, what's wrong?"

"Rashawn doesn't want to play with me anymore. He said I don't give him any credit."

"Basketball is a team sport. Although you scored the game-winning points, Rashawn still played his part in helping to win the game. Try including him in the celebration."

Steadman thinks about all the many days of practice he and Rashawn did after school. He realizes that Rashawn scored points, got rebounds, and played defense in the game.

Steadman runs back into the cafeteria and grabs the microphone next to the podium by the fruit trays. "Everyone, I have an announcement. I did score the game-winning points, but without Rashawn's help, we could not have won the game. Thank you, Rashawn, for all that you did!"

Rashawn's eyes grow wide, and a big smile spreads across his furry face. He runs to Steadman and hugs him. "Thank you, Steadman, and yes, I will play with you next year!"

"We did it! Together, we won the game!" they shout.

The End

Meet Jeffrey Roy Ford

Jeffrey Roy Ford is an animal lover and former substitute teacher. He has dedicated his life to making a difference by using his love for animals to create fun stories that teach children important life lessons.

CPSIA information can be obtained
at www.ICGtesting.com
Printed in the USA
JSHW041222150323
38949JS00002B/9